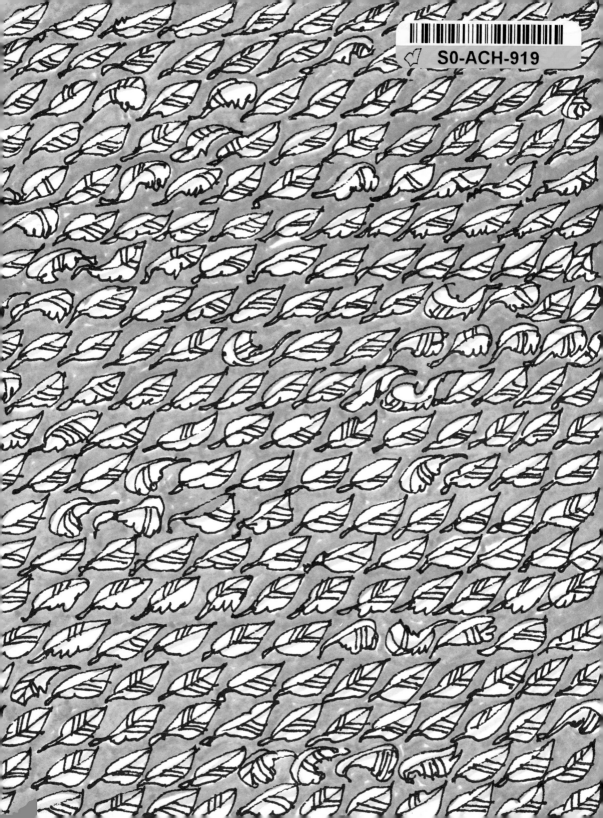

Mouse Feathers

by Robert Quackenbush

CLARION BOOKS

TICKNOR & FIELDS: A HOUGHTON MIFFLIN COMPANY

NEW YORK

Clarion Books
Ticknor & Fields, a Houghton Mifflin Company
Text and illustrations copyright © 1988 by Robert M. Quackenbush

Library of Congress Cataloging-in-Publication Data
Quackenbush, Robert M.
Mouse feathers.
Summary: While Maxine Mouse babysits her two
nephews, a pillow fight gets out of control and the
nephews come down with bad cases of "Mouse Feathers."
[1. Baby sitters—Fiction.   2. Mice—Fiction]   I. Title.
PZ7.Q16Mou   1988   [E]   87-15690
ISBN 0-89919-527-X

Y 10 9 8 7 6 5 4 3 2 1

On the day
Maxine Mouse's little nephews
were dropped off at her house
to be baby-sat,
they got into a
terrible pillow fight.

One of the pillows
tore open.
Feathers went flying
everywhere.
"Stop!" cried Maxine.

Maxine's nephews didn't
hear her.
They were having too much
fun laughing and giggling
and fighting with the pillows.
Then the other pillow broke.
Maxine ran to close
the windows
to keep the feathers
from flying.

Suddenly, Maxine
remembered her
freshly painted bedroom.
What if the feathers
got in the paint?
She raced down the hall
to close the bedroom door.

Too late!
There were feathers
stuck to the walls
and ceiling
and all over
the woodwork.

Maxine ran back
into the living room.
"Stop!" she cried again.
But her nephews
were laughing and
giggling more than ever
and didn't hear her.
Maxine chased after them,
but it did no good.

Then Maxine remembered
the dough she had made
that morning to bake bread.
It was rising in a
bowl on the kitchen table
next to a freshly iced cake.
Maxine ran to the kitchen
to cover them.

Too late!
Feathers had gotten in
the dough and
in the icing.
Maxine tried to remove
the feathers.
She got sticky dough
and icing all over herself
and the kitchen.

That did it!
Sticky fingers and all, Maxine
ran into the living room and
wrestled the pillows away
from her nephews.
She got feathers stuck
all over herself, but at
least she got the pillows!
Now she had the job of
cleaning up the feathers.
She ran to get the
vacuum cleaner.

Maxine lugged the heavy
vacuum cleaner into the living room.
But when she turned it on,
she pushed the wrong button.
Air came rushing out
of the machine
—not in, as it should.
Maxine fumbled for the switch.

Too late!
Feathers were flying
about worse than ever.
"It's snowing!" shouted Maxine's
nephews happily. "Let's
build a snowman!"

At last, Maxine
was able to shut off
the vacuum cleaner.
The feathers stopped flying.
The nephews stopped playing.
All was very quiet.
Too quiet.
"We're sick," moaned
the nephews.

Maxine wondered
what to do.
Her nephews' parents
were at the theater
and couldn't be reached.
What if the children
had some dreadful disease?
Maxine ran to the phone
and called a doctor.

The doctor
came at once
and examined
Maxine's nephews.
"What's wrong with them,
Doctor?" pleaded Maxine.
"A very unusual case,"
replied the doctor.
"My diagnosis is
that your nephews have…

..... Mouse Feathers!

But they'll be over it in a jiffy."